Lena Anderson

Stina

Greenwillow Books

NEW YORK

Every summer Stina visited her grandfather
in his house by the sea.

And every summer she went treasure hunting.
Smooth sticks, sea glass, feathers—there
was so much to be found.

Stina and her grandfather always got up
early in the morning.

Grandpa liked to drink his coffee outside.
On calm mornings, the sea was so shiny it looked
as if it had just been painted.

After breakfast they went out in
Grandpa's boat to check the nets.

Sometimes the nets were full of fish.
Sometimes there was nothing but a bit of seaweed.

"We did well today," said Grandpa as he
hung up the net. "One turbot,
two perch, and four flounders."

"I'm doing well, too," said Stina, who had
just found a fine seagull feather.

Grandpa kept some of the fish
they caught in a net in the water.

Every evening Stina pulled it out of the
water and chose a fish for dinner.

It was always delicious.

After dinner Grandpa made himself
a pot of coffee.

Sometimes Stina washed the dishes
as a surprise.

In the evening they listened to the
weather report on the radio.

One night there was a storm warning.
"Did you hear that, Stina?" asked Grandpa.
"We're in for a real blow."

When Grandpa came to kiss Stina good night,
her bed was empty!

He rushed out of the house calling
"Stina, Stina!"

Grandpa found Stina sitting on a rock, crying.

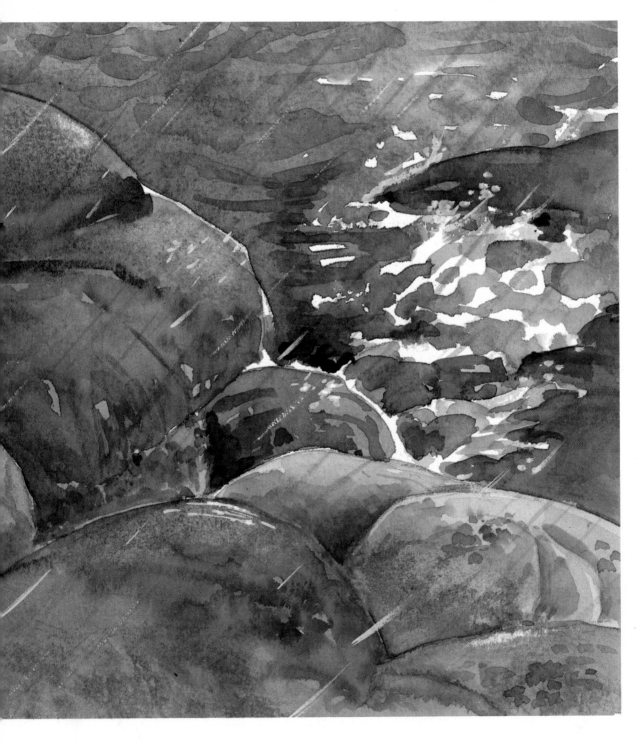

"I came out to see the storm," she said.
"But I don't like it."

Grandpa picked her up and hugged her.

"Dear child," he said, "this is no way to see
a storm. You're soaking wet and so am I.
Let's go inside and start all over again."

"If you're going to go out in a storm there should
be at least two of you," said Grandpa.

"And you should be properly dressed.
    Let's go."

Grandpa and Stina watched the rain beating
down and the waves breaking on the rocks.

"I like it better now," said Stina. "And look
what the storm has brought me."

"When I go home, may I take the storm's present
with me, Grandpa?" asked Stina.

"I don't see why not," said Grandpa.

And that's exactly what she did!